Some Folk Think the South Pole's Hot

Some Folk Think the South Pole's Hot

The Three Tenors Play the Antarctic

by Elke Heidenreich
pictures by Quint Buchholz
translated by Aubrey M. Woolman

DAVID R. GODINE, Publisher

First English edition published in 2001 by
David R. Godine, Publisher, Inc.
Post Office Box 450
Jaffrey, New Hampshire 03452
www.godine.com

LIBRARY OF CONGRESS CATALOGING-IN-PUBLICATION DATA
Heidenreich, Elke.
[Am Südpol, denkt man, ist es heiß. English]
Some folk think the South Pole's hot /
by Elke Heidenreich ; illustrations by Quint Buchholz ;
translated by Aubrey M. Woolman. — 1st American ed.
p. cm.
Summary: The penguins of the South Pole, all dressed up
and with no place to go, invite the Three Tenors to
come and perform an opera for their amusement.
ISBN: 1—56792—170—1 (alk. paper)
[1. Penguins—Fiction. 2. South Pole—Fiction.
3. Opera—Fiction. 4. Singers—Fiction.
5. Carreras, José—Fiction.
6. Domingo, Plácido, 1941— — Fiction
7. Pavarotti, Luciano—Fiction.
8. Stories in rhyme.]
I. Buchholz, Quint, ill. II. Woolman, Aubrey M.
III. Title.
PZ8.3.H4125 So 2001
[E]—dc21 00-061000

FIRST EDITION 2001
Printed and bound in Spain by Bookprint, S.L. Barcelona

for
P.D., J.C. and L.P.

Some folk think
the South Pole's hot.

With ice and snow?

Of course it's not!

It's home, though, to those handsome birds,

The penguins – creatures of few words. . .

Two hundred thousand, at a guess,
Maybe more, or slightly less.

To count so many, can't be done —
You'll find there father, mother, son,
Daughter, grandma, cousin, aunt,
One can't tell which, though, that I grant.
No fear have they of winter storm:
They have fur coats to keep them warm.

(Fur coats indeed — a luxury rare,
Surely it's feathers most birds wear?
A downy coat young birds prefer,
Could be feathers, could be fur.
But since you ask, I shall confess
The penguins' smart and natty dress
Consists of feathers, densely matted —
A pity they can't be top-hatted!)

WHERE WAS I? Penguins feel no cold,
They stand and chat of days of old,
Of how things were in times long past
And wonder if the ice will last.
Or, should a colder spell be due
Would Grandpa Walter see it through?
And could they keep the children warm?
...Well, Charles, at least runs true to form:
Came crawling home the other night
Down on all fours, he was so tight.
In short:
When long the night and cold the day,
They gossip to pass the time away!

They are, I'd say, a splendid sight,
In evening dress, both day and night.
(Well, just the adult is so smart,
The fluffy chick, God bless its heart,
Is still too cuddly, young and tender,
One cannot even tell its gender.
Perhaps in protest or revolt
One day this hopeful starts to moult
And through its covering of down —
Hard to believe, I have to own —
One glimpses its black evening dress,
Still looking somewhat of a mess!)

ALL PENGUINS, as I said, wear tails
(Or evening dress), not just the males.
You're puzzled by this craze for fashion
And ask the reason for their passion:
Why do they like to be such smarties,
Is it because they love posh parties?
Fat chance! For, as you know,
All they have is ice and snow;
Yet ev'ry penguin learns at school
Looking elegant is 'cool':
One never knows if, without warning,
A steamship might arrive one morning.

Sometimes in summer or in spring,
One will appear and new hope bring.
Once, in three years or four,
It comes, but sends no fuel ashore,
Nor lands it tourists for a greeting —
They'd only freeze there without heating.
(They think: South Pole? Must be hot!
Snow and ice? That they forgot.)
Why, there's a ship approaching now,
Breaking through the ice somehow.

Now, really, there's no need to panic,
It won't meet the fate of the *Titanic*!
Hark! One can't mistake *that* tenor:

It's the Opera Ship from Old Vienna.

An Opera Ship? What do they plan, O,
'Mid snow and ice? They've brought a piano,
Violins, too, clarinets and drums,
Such music ne'er to the South Pole comes,
And look! Do eyes deceive?

THE THREE TENORS, I do believe!

It really is all three of them.
On shore, the scene is pure mayhem
As penguins, overcome with joy,
Go wild, with shouts of 'Ship ahoy!'
Though penguins are so smartly dressed,
That they love opera, who'd have guessed?
The tenors, though, their season done,
Think the South Pole might be fun!
(Since truthful I have always been,
It's time, I think, that I came clean:
When no one offers you a role,
Your only choice is the South Pole!
It should have been a secret kept,
To blurt it out may seem inept,
Still, out is out, or so they say,
And everyone's found out some day.)

As I was saying, on opera keen,
The penguins hope they'll play *Undine*.
She's the water sprite who craves
A human child but, 'mong the waves,
A cruel fate meets. (As you supposed,
This opera's the one Lortzing composed.)
Perhaps *Aïda* they'll present
Or to *The Magic Flute* consent.
The penguins' hearts are all a-flutter,
For love and joy turn them to butter.
(You don't believe that penguins, too,
Can love the way that humans do?
Well, humans fall in love, of course,
But once they're married soon divorce.
Human love grows quickly stale,

While penguins' love does long prevail.
Pairs stay together, it appears,
For many, many, many years.
Both hatch the eggs, both feed the chicks,
Share happiness and Fate's cruel tricks.
Ever faithful, they cling together,
Upon their rock, whate'er the weather.
They shield their chicks and watch them grow,
And keep them safe, come wind, come snow.
They teach them flying, swimming, diving,
They climb the smoothest ice, surviving,
And being ever positive,
An apology they're quick to give,
Should they an angry word let slip.)

As I was saying, the Opera Ship
Is anchored at the South Pole now,
A notice board hung from its prow,
And little Leo just can't wait
To row out and investigate.
The only penguin who can read,
A clever child is he, indeed.
His parents never forced the lad,
But, of course, are proud and glad:
'Quite like Einstein in his day,
Young Leo is,' they often say.

Such chances don't come every week,
So, with glasses on his beak,
To read the notice Leo's willing
And what it says is truly thrilling:

'From Vienna comes this Opera Ship,
Making a very special trip
To greet all penguins. For your delight,
An opera we'll perform tonight.
Written by Verdi, long ago,
An opera that you'll love, we know.
It tells the story of Violetta
Who loves Alfredo, her social better.
We soon find out that there's a catch:
His father disapproves the match.
Violetta's forced to swear an oath
To leave Alfredo, though much loth.
So each then leads a lonely life,
She's no husband, he's no wife.
The end is sad, there's no denying,
Alfredo finds Violetta dying,
Coughing, she falls into his arms,
While he, distressed, sings of her charms.
But though she dies as the curtain draws,
We hope for your prolonged applause.'

Below was written, half hidden by ice,
The opera's name and ticket price.
La Traviata it was, you've guessed.
The Three Tenors would give their best:
Carreras would Alfredo bring
And Domingo would the father sing,
While Violetta, sweet and tender,
None but Pavarotti could render!

Young Leo now rows back to land
To announce the program that's been planned.
The tickets soon are selling fast
And the long, long line moves slowly past.
But penguins who don't want to stand
Find Leo tickets has to hand.
Where he got them, no one knows!
(They're a little dearer, I suppose.)
Yes, this young Leo's got it made,
He cheats a bit I am afraid,
Hoping, no doubt, that he'll get rich.
His plumage is as black as pitch,
Or, some would say, as black as night,
With just a tiny flash of white
On the wing tips. That's why, you know,
They've nicknamed him Penguin Nero.

WHERE WAS I? Yes, young Leo's wiles,
The ticket line stretches out for miles.
Old Walter, by the long wait tired,
At last two tickets has acquired.
But as he totters home to tea
One flies away into the sea.

In vain he tries to rescue it,
But for such antics he's not fit.
Red with rage, he foresees strife
If he's a ticket but *not* his wife!

This penguin here is little Lotti,
Who thinks that opera-going is dotty.
She can't see why to go's a duty
And finds all opera-goers snooty.
Her mother sobs, her father's mad,
And Uncle Otto says she's bad:
'What's the use of raising chicks?
What else is there to do here? Nix!
A ship arrives with Pavarotti,
Who doesn't want to hear him? Lotti!
If you don't brush your feathers now
And come with me, there'll be a row.'
Otto was mad, Lotti could tell,
For once he'd played the violin well.

But months ago, one freezing night,
His violin shattered. Sad was his plight!
No sun for him since then has shone,
But there's no help. What's gone is gone.
At night he roams from place to place
Carrying his empty violin case,
And loudly lamenting, 'Oh dear, oh!
I miss my lovely violin so!'

But Lotti finds her uncle mean,
Though ne'er an opera has she seen.
The violin she just can't stand,
But thinks the Spice Girls simply grand.
Otto cries, 'Not ready yet?'
The nest with mother's tears is wet.
In short, there is a great kerfuffle,
Then darkness falls, the sounds to muffle.
The ship is now ablaze with light
And penguins run to see the sight.
How happy and how smart they look,
Like models in a fashion book!
(Dressed to sartorial perfection,
I envy them their clothes selection.
When for an opera I want to dress,
In a wardrobe full, I must confess
There's nothing fit for Richard Strauss!)

Where was I? Ah, the opera house,
Or Opera Ship, it's out there now
Brightly lit from stern to bow.
The excitement reaches fever pitch,
When a trumpet call, piercing but rich,
Bursts upon the South Pole night,
To penguins' cries of sheer delight.

The performance starts at eight o'clock,
So the penguins to the sea all flock,
All except one broody pair
Who for their baby chicks must care.
But Leo has purloined a boat –
With feathers it's quite hard to float.
Just look how beautif'ly they dive
To be first aboard they strive!
The sight is one I'll not forget –
But won't their evening dress get wet?
(No, it's sure to be well greased,
In fact, it won't get even creased.)

Now, in a flash, as you can check,
They leap aboard on to the deck.
(Could your parents, thin or fat,
Leap in evening dress like that?)

WHERE WAS I? The opera soon will start,
How fast now beats a penguin's heart!
As all the penguins go below,
What happens the next pages show:
Here, to a wonderland transformed,
The opera's about to be performed.

Se non è vero
è molto ben trova*

The walls are painted all in gold,
A scene most wond'rous to behold.
The handsome crystal chandelier,
With all its candles, one might fear,
Could give the penguins palpitations –
They're not used to such illuminations!
The curtain is of velvet red,
The seats are soft as any bed.
All sink in them with great relief,
Mother needs her handkerchief.
Father quickly cleans his ear,
Uncle wipes his glasses clear.
Leo's in the second row,
Lotti's with him, too, you know.
While others swam, you should take note,
She came with Leo in the boat.
And everyone's in evening dress,
No one in jeans to cause distress,
Unlike the opera in Cologne,
Where none have smart clothes of their own.

WHERE WAS I? Everyone is here,
Should the conductor not appear?
Ah, here he is. He gives a bow,
Then waves his arms. O, come on now!

42

He lifts his baton — talk no more:
Here is
        the moment
                we're waiting for!

As the candles are slowly extinguished,
A hush falls on the darkened theater
And the conductor, a musician distinguished,
Starts the music: heav'n couldn't be better!

For the penguins, there's no music finer
And this, of course, is before the first act.
Marked 'Adagio' and in B minor,
It melts ev'ry heart, and that's a fact!

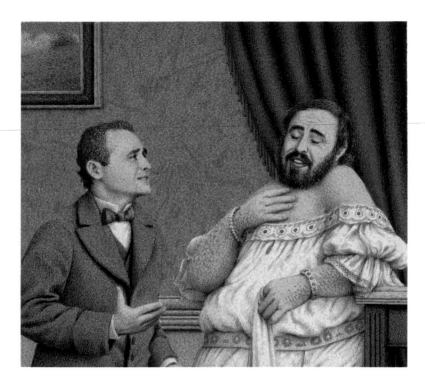

Soon their tears begin to freely flow,
For penguins are such tender-hearted birds,
They only weep if no one's near to know
And never put their feelings into words.

The curtain rises, a gay party scene,
It's Paris, Violetta's elegant salon,
Love (and Fate) are not slow to intervene,
But no one thinks, 'Now happiness has gone.'

The penguins listen with intense emotion
As Alfredo sings his aria praising love.
Though of Paris they have never a notion,
Love means more to them than to a turtle dove.

When Violetta sings, 'No more of sorrow,'
For 'tis to joyful tidings that she leans,
Inviting guests who see a bright tomorrow,
All penguins know exactly what she means.

Who doesn't wish to lead a life of pleasure?
Who doesn't yearn for luck in large amounts?
South Pole penguins like New Yorkers treasure
Happiness and love, they're all that counts.

'Ah, moments of snatched happiness soon vanish,
And present dreams do not last many moons.'
Thus sings Alfredo's father, out to banish
All thoughts of love. Then Violetta swoons.

Now ev'ry penguin really *is* in tears
And even Lotti has to wipe her eyes,
While tough young Leo, too, so it appears,
Is moved as he looks 'round in shocked surprise.

And yet there's worse to come, as we all know.
Violetta's broken-hearted, full of care.
But now Alfredo rushes in and so
Can love, we wonder, triumph o'er despair?

His deep concern Alfredo cannot hide
As in his arms Violetta tries to rise;
Ah, Fate's all-powerful will won't be denied.
Wracked by a coughing fit, alas, she dies.

Yet in the very end she clings to life,
'I feel returning strength,' she sings, 'O, joy!'
Still hoping she can be Alfredo's wife,
A hope that death will all too soon destroy.

Alfredo weeps, but will, no doubt, recover.
We know that time all pain can soothe away.
It's true he can't be Violetta's lover
And that his grief will yet last many a day,

But in the end the sun will shine once more
And laughter will replace Alfredo's pain.
No tears can lost loved ones restore,
Not at the South Pole, Texas, or Maine.

The music fades upon the final scene,
The curtain rustles, then all is still;
When pleased, penguins can't clap their hands
So they clap their wings, and do it with a will.

'Bravo!' they shout and jump for joy so high
The captain fears the ship may well capsize,
'Come back, Three Tenors,' excitedly they cry,
'Encore, encore!' and praise them to the skies.

Our tenors can't believe that at the Pole,
So rapturous a reception they'd receive,
For in Madrid (let's call it an own goal)
By hecklers they were forced the stage to leave.

Now Pavarotti's loth to disengage
Himself from calls for more and more encores.
We see him running back on to the stage,
Waving his handkerchief to more applause.

But all in vain — as ev'ry penguin knows,
When the lights go up, the opera's reached its close.

And so, their eyes with tears abrim,
The birds begin their homeward swim.
In the water, wings a-flapping,
Some of them just can't stop clapping.
They want to stay and plead in vain,
'We'd like to see it all again.'
They'd give, they say, most anything
To hear again Alfredo sing.
And Pavarotti they must kiss.
(But that, no doubt, they'll have to miss!)
They clap, they sing, they cheer, they shout
Till Pavarotti once more comes out,
Waving his famous handkerchief:
'Enough!' he cries. It's past belief.
Radiantly happy, full of pride,
Exhausted, he then steps inside.

For penguins, it all seems a dream
From which they wake to see the gleam
Of golden walls. That must be wrong!
They've aching backs, they've sat too long.
For them a chair is like a vice,
And they're so hot! Back to the ice!
The penguins then, no time to lose,
Climb back on deck in ones and twos,
While high above the moon shines bright,
And *that*, at least, they know is right.

Young Leo, too, rows back to shore,
Beside him Lotti, who'd want more?
We might have guessed right from the start
That she'd become Leo's sweetheart.
He asks her how she liked the show,
She says, 'It wasn't bad, although
The Spice Girls' songs are brill and shorter.'
As they glide homeward through the water,
Bold Leo whispers in her ear,
'Next April, they are coming here.'
Then Lotti, asking, 'Is that true?'
Gives him a kiss. He's earned it, too!
'They'll come,' boasts Leo, 'leave that to me.'
Thinking, we'll just wait and see.
By then, he reckons — he's really rotten —
Spice Girls *and* tenors will be forgotten.

Now it is night. Tired penguins yawn.
The sea is calm, peace reigns till dawn.
The penguins, standing in the snow,
Miss the lovely music so.
In their hearts, love's flame still burns.
Each for another opera yearns.
The Opera ship is coming back!
Of that they're sure as black is black,
And then they'll be already dressed
In evening clothes, as you'll have guessed.
But till it comes, till that glad date,
They cannot idly stand and wait:
They've fish to catch and chicks to feed,
Fear for the future. Oh yes, indeed,
For to the North, the South, the West,
Nowhere does Nature look its best.

As global warming melts the ice,
The penguins' prospect isn't nice.
But yet they put aside their fear:
'Aïda,' they swear, 'we'd love to hear.'
A chance, we hope, that soon occurs,
For now we know they're connoisseurs.

WHERE WAS I?
                    Yes.

                              It's been great fun.

But now, goodbye!
                    The book
                              is done.

59

P.S.

You liked the book? Then buy it, please,
Quint and I need the royalties.
Need them for what, you well may ask,
To lie on a crowded beach and bask
In the scorching sun and then get cool
In a luxury hotel swimming pool?
No, no! You smile, I think you've guessed,
What both of us would like the best:
To visit the South Pole, there to see
The penguins in reality.
They are, of course, our fav'rite birds.
That's why I've written all these words,
And Quint has painted them so well,
I'm sure the book is going to sell.
Then with the money that you pay
To the South Pole we'll be away,
There bring to life this color print

Of Elke

a penguin

and Quint!

ELKE HEIDENREICH, born in 1934, studied German literature and theater arts in Munich, Hamburg, and Berlin. For many years she was involved in the production of radio and television broadcasts: as moderator on talk shows such as *Cologne Meetingplace* and *Live from the Opera*, and as program director of *Literature Club* on Swiss television, among others. She has her own column in the magazine *Brigitte* and is a regular commentator for *Brigitte TV*. The author of numerous television plays and series, a stage play, and the screenplay *When Winter Comes* (with Bernd Schroeder), Elke Heidenreich has also written several books, including *Nero Corleone*, illustrated by Quint Buchholz. She lives with her husband in Cologne.

Born in 1957, QUINT BUCHHOLZ initially studied art history, and later painting and graphic arts at the Academy of Fine Arts in Munich. Since 1988 he has illustrated and designed numerous books and has provided illustrations for a large number of book jackets. Among his recent projects are the illustrations for *Matti and His Grandfather* by Robert Piumini and *The Collector of Moments*, named an Outstanding Children's Book by the *New York Times* in 1999.

Some Folk Think
the South Pole's Hot

has been set in a digital version of Frederic Goudy's Deepdene.
Designed for Monotype composition in 1927, Deepdene bears
a distinct family resemblance to the types Goudy designed for
hand composition, yet is free of the short descenders that mar
some of the faces he designed for machine composition. Frankly
decorative in their details, both the roman and the italic (like
many of Goudy's types) recall his early experience as a designer
of letters for advertising and magazines, as well as his abiding
interest in the types created at the height of the fine press move-
ment of the late nineteenth and early twentieth centuries.
Notable for its spontaneous drawing and strong vertical
emphasis, Deepdene is considered one of
Goudy's most successful faces.

Composition and layout by
Carl W. Scarbrough

+ +
+